BUMSTEAD

BUMSTEAD

Within the fairy-tale treasury which has come into the world's possession, there is no doubt Hans Christian Andersen's stories are of outstanding character. Their symbolism is rich with Christian values, and some of them are clear illustrations of the Gospel. From his early childhood in the town of Odense, Denmark, until his death in Copenhagen, Hans Christian Andersen (1805-1875) had a valid Christian faith that manifest itself in many of the approximately 150 stories and tales he wrote. In one of them he said: "In every human life, whether poor or great, there is an invisible thread that shows we belong to God." The thread in Andersen's stories is one of optimism that has given hope and inspiration to people all over the world.

It is in this spirit that Scandinavia Fairy Tales are published. We are convinced of the validity of teaching spiritual principles and building character values through imaginative stories, just as Jesus used parables to teach the people of His time.

LITTLE CLAUS AND BIG CLAUS
by Hans Christian Andersen
Translated from the original Danish text by
Terence Andrew Day BA
Illustrated by Francois Crozat
U.S. edition 1988 by WORD Inc. Waco, TX 76702
Text: © Copyright 1987 Scandinavia Publishing House,
Nørregade 32, DK-1165, Copenhagen K, Denmark
Artwork: © Copyright 1987 Francois Crozat and
Scandinavia Publishing House
Printed in Hong Kong
ISBN 0-8499-8541-2

Hans Christian Andersen

Little Claus
and Big Claus

Translated for children
from the original Danish text
by Terence Andrew Day BA
Illustrated by Francois Crozat

WORD INC.

3

Once upon a time, there were two men in a village who both had the same name. They were called Claus. Their only difference was, one owned four horses and the other owned one horse. People in the village called the one with four horses Big Claus and the one with the one horse Little Claus. Now let's hear what happened to them, because this is really a true story!

All week long, Little Claus had to plow for Big Claus and lend him his one horse; then Big Claus helped him in return with his four horses, but only once a week, and that was on Sunday.

Yipee! How Little Claus cracked his whip over all five horses on Sunday. On that one day it was just as if they all belonged to him. The sun shone brightly and all the bells in the church tower were ringing.

People were dressed in their Sunday best, holding their hymn-books under their arms walking on their way to hear the parson preach. They looked at Little Claus who was plowing with the five horses. He was so pleased with himself that he cracked his whip once more, shouting, "Gee-up my five horses!"

"You mustn't say that," said Big Claus, "it's only the one horse that belongs to you!"

But as soon as the next person passed by, Little Claus forgot and shouted, "Gee-up my five horses!"

"Right then, now you've got to stop it!" Big Claus said, "otherwise I'll hit your horse on the head and it will fall down dead, right on the spot. Then that will be the end of him!"

"I promise I won't ever say it again!" said Little Claus.

But as soon as some people came along, nodding, "Good day," he felt so proud to have five horses plowing his field, that he cracked his whip and shouted, "Gee-up my five horses!"

"I'll gee-up your horses for you, just you see!" said Big Claus, and taking hold of a huge mallet, he bashed Little Claus's only horse on the head, so it fell over in an instant, as dead as a doornail.

"Oh no! Now I haven't got any horse at all!" said Little Claus. And he began to cry.

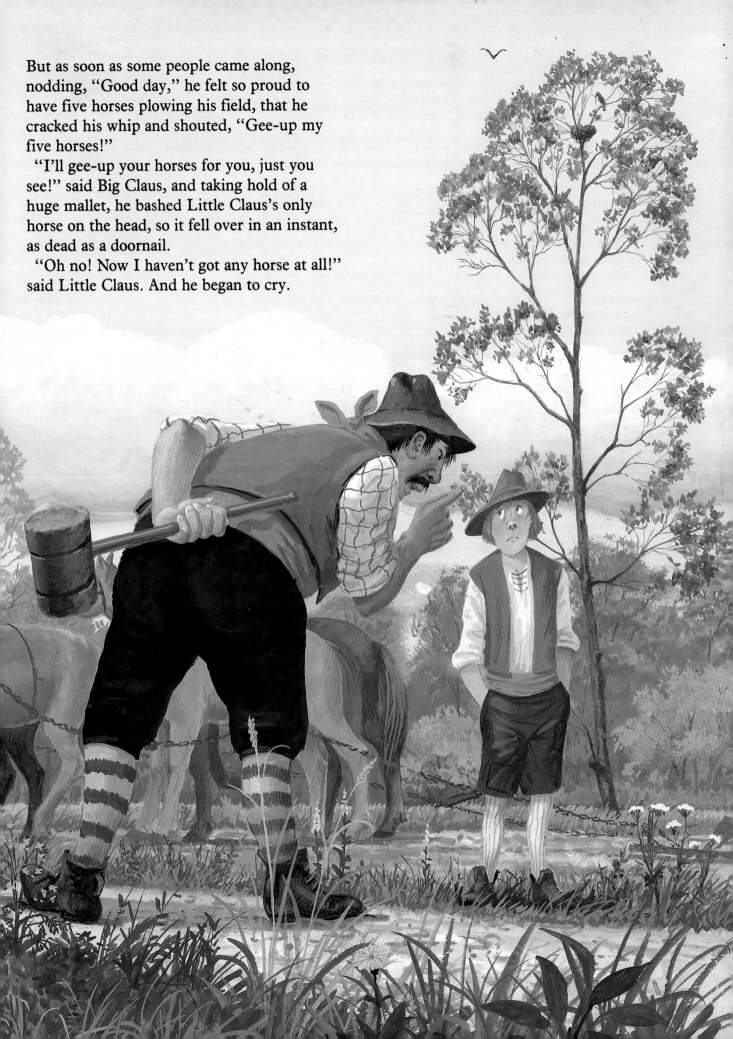

After some time he skinned the horse, took the hide and hung it out to dry in the wind. He then put the horse-skin in a sack, swung it over his shoulder and started toward town, where he could sell his horse-skin.

He had ever such a long way to go, and had to pass through a great, dark wood and a terrible storm was blowing. He lost his way completely. By the time he came upon the right path it was well into the evening and both the town and his home were too far away for him to reach before it grew dark.

Near the road there stood a big farmhouse, the shutters outside the windows were closed, but light could still be seen shining through the cracks. "Maybe they'll let me stay the night," thought Little Claus. He went over to the door and knocked.

The farmer's wife opened the door, but when she heard what he wanted, she told him to go on his way, as her husband was not at home and she did not let in any strangers.

"Oh well, then I'll just have to lie out here," said Little Claus and the farmer's wife slammed the door in his face.

Nearby stood a large haystack and between it and the house was a little shed with a flat thatched roof.

"I can lie up there!" said Little Claus when he saw the roof, "that will make me a lovely bed, though I hope that stork won't fly down and peck my feet." For indeed, a stork had made its nest on top of the roof.

Little Claus climbed up onto the shed and lay down. While he tossed and turned to get really comfortable, he noticed that because the wooden shutters did not cover the windows at the top, he could see right into the living room.

A large table was set with wine, roast meat and delicious fish. The farmer's wife and the church deacon were sitting at the table by themselves. She was pouring him a glass of wine and he was helping himself to the fish, which he liked very much.

"I wish I could have some of that, too!" said Little Claus, stretching his head towards the window. Heavens! What a lovely cake he could see there! It was a real feast!

Suddenly he heard someone riding down the road towards the house. It was the woman's husband returning home.

He was normally a very nice man, but had the unusual illness of not being able to stand the sight of church deacons. If he saw a deacon, he would go raging mad. And that was why the church deacon had dropped by to pay the farmer's wife a visit, knowing her husband would not be at home. The good woman gave the deacon all the best food in the house, but when she heard her husband coming, she and the deacon became frightened. The woman begged the deacon to hide in a large empty chest, which was standing in the corner. This he did, for he knew full well that her husband could not stand the sight of deacons.

Quickly the wife put away all the lovely food and wine into the oven, for if her husband saw it, he would be sure to ask what it meant.

"Oh well," sighed Little Claus on top of the shed as he saw all the food being put away.

"Is there someone up there?" the farmer asked, looking up at Little Claus. "What are you lying up there for? You're welcome to come inside with me!"

So Little Claus told him how he had lost his way and asked if he might stay the night.

"Of course you can!" said the farmer, "but first let's have something to eat!"

The woman received them both very kindly, laid a cloth on a long table and gave them a large dish of porridge. The farmer was hungry and ate with a good appetite, but Little Claus could not stop thinking of the delicious roast meat, fish and cake he knew were in the oven.

Underneath the table, at his feet he had laid his sack containing the horse-skin. For as you know, he had left home to sell it in town. He did not like the porridge and so began stepping on his sack so the dry skin in it made a loud squeaking noise.

"Shh!" said Little Claus to his sack, while he continued rubbing his foot against the skin so it squeaked even more.

"Hello! what you got in your sack?" asked the farmer.

"Oh, it's a magician!" said Little Claus, "he says we don't have to eat porridge as he has

magically filled the oven with roast meat, fish and cake."

"You don't say!" said the farmer. He rushed over to open the oven. There he found all the delicious food his wife had hidden, but which he now believed the magician in the sack had made for them. The wife dared not say anything, but straight away set the food on the table, and so both of them ate the fish, the roast meat and the cake. Then Little Claus trod on his sack again, making the horse-skin squeak.

"What's he saying now?" asked the farmer.

"He says," said Little Claus, "that he has also conjured up three bottles of wine for us and they are also in the oven!"

So the wife had to bring out the wine she had hidden and the farmer drank until he became quite merry. He wished he could have a magician like the one Little Claus had in his sack.

"Can he also conjure up the devil?" asked the farmer, "I'd like to see him now that I'm having such a good time!"

"Sure!" said Little Claus, "my magician can do anything I tell him to, isn't that right?" he asked, stepping on the sack so it squeaked. "Can you hear him? He says "yes." But I'm afraid you won't like the look of him, he's terribly ugly."

"Oh, I'm not scared at all, what's he look like?"

"Well, he'll appear as the spitting image of a church deacon!"

"Yuk!" said the farmer, "that **is** ugly! You must know that I cannot bear the sight of church deacons! But that doesn't matter now, since I know it's the devil, I won't mind so much! Now I'm really feeling brave! But don't let him get too close to me."

"Now I will ask my magician," said Little Claus. He stepped on the sack and stooped down to hear better.

"What's he saying?"

"He says you are to go over to the chest in the corner and open it. There you will see the devil squatting inside, but you must keep a hold of the lid so he doesn't slip out."

"Will you help me hold on to it?" asked the farmer. He went over to the chest where his wife had hidden the real deacon, who was inside and really very frightened.

The farmer lifted the lid a little and peeked inside.

"Yuk!" he cried and sprang backwards. "Yes you're right, he looked exactly like our church deacon! It was awful!"

This called for another drink and so they drank until quite late that night.

"You must sell me that magician," said the farmer. "Ask for whatever you want! I'll give you a whole bushel of money here and now!"

"No, I can't do that!" said Little Claus, "just think how useful this magician is to me!"

"Oh, please, I really would like to have him, ever so much," said the farmer. He kept on pleading with Little Claus.

"Well, all right," said Little Claus at last, "seeing as you've been so kind as to give me a place to sleep tonight, I'll let you have him. You can have the magician for a bushel of money filled to the brim."

"I'll give it you right away," said the farmer, "but you'll have to take that chest there with you before you go, I'm not having it in the house a moment longer, there's no way of knowing whether he's still lurking in there or not."

So Little Claus gave the farmer his sack with the dried horse-skin inside and in return, he received a whole bushel of money, filled right to the brim. The farmer also let him have a large wheelbarrow to carry away the money and the chest.

"Good-bye!" said Little Claus pushing along the wheelbarrow with his money and the large chest in which the deacon was still hiding.

On the other side of the woods was a wide, deep river, the water flowed with such speed that you could hardly swim against the strength of the current. Not too long ago a large bridge had been built across it and in the middle of this bridge Little Claus stopped and said out loud so the deacon in the chest could hear him. "Well, what am I going to do with this stupid chest? It's so heavy, you'd think there were stones in it! Wheeling this chest about is tiring me out, so I'll just push it into the river, if the current carries it back to my house, that's fine, if it doesn't, then it's all the same, it makes no difference to me."

So he took hold of the chest with one hand and began to lift it, just as if he were going to shove it into the water.

"No, don't do that!" shrieked the deacon inside the chest, "just let me out!"

"Ohhhhh!" said Little Claus, pretending to be frightened. "He's still in there! I'll have to push it in the river right away, so he'll drown!"

"Oh no, oh no!" yelled the deacon, "I'll give you a whole bushelful of money if you let me go!"

"Well that's a different matter!" said Little Claus and opened the chest.

The deacon crawled out as fast as he could and shoved the empty chest into the river. Then he went home to fetch a bushelful of money which he gave to Little Claus who already had one bushel full from the farmer. Now Little Claus's wheelbarrow was full of money!

"Look at this, I've really been paid well for my horse!" he said to himself when he got home to his own room, dumping a huge heap of money onto the floor.

"That will really make Big Claus mad when he finds out how rich I've become because of my one horse, but I won't tell him the whole story!"

He sent a boy over to Big Claus's to borrow a bushel. "I wonder what he wants with that!" thought Big Claus. So he smeared the bottom of the bushel with tar. That way whatever Little Claus put in the bushel, some of it would stay stuck inside. Sure enough, when he got his bushel back, there were three silver coins stuck to the bottom.

"What's going on?" said Big Claus. He ran straight over to Little Claus. "Where did you get all that money from?"

"Oh, I got that for my horse-skin I sold yesterday!"

"You were paid well for that, I must say!" said Big Claus who then ran home, took an axe and killed all four of his horses, took their skins and went off into town to sell them.

"Get your horse-skins here! Horse-skins! Who'll buy my lovely horse-skins?" He cried as he went along the streets. All the shoemakers and tanners came running and asked how much he was willing to sell them for.

"A bushel of money each!" said Big Claus.

"Are you nuts, or something?" they all said, "I suppose you think we've got bushels of money?"

"Get your skins here! Horse-skins! Who'll buy my lovely horse-skins?" He kept on shouting, but everyone who asked what the skins cost, were told, "a bushelful of money."

"He wants to make fools of us," they all said. So the shoemakers took their straps and the tanners their leather aprons and they began beating Big Claus.

"Horse-skins, Horse-skins!" they all jeered at him. "We'll give you a real good hiding! Get out of town!" they shouted, and Big Claus had to make off at topspeed, he had never before taken such a thrashing from anyone.

"Just you wait!" he said when he got home, "Little Claus will pay for this, I'm going to kill him!"

Meanwhile at Little Claus's home, his old grandmother had just died. Even though she had been rather nasty and unkind to him, he nevertheless felt upset and so he took the dead woman and laid her in his own warm bed to see whether she could come back to life again. She spent all night in his bed while Little Claus sat over in the corner and slept in a chair as he had often done before.

During the night the door opened and in came Big Claus with an axe in his hand. He knew exactly where to find Little Claus's bed. He went over to it and struck the dead grandmother on the head, thinking it was Little Claus.

"Take that!" he said, "You won't be playing any more tricks on me now!" Then he went on his way again.

"What a wicked and evil man!" said Little Claus.

"He meant to kill me. It was a good thing Grandmother was already dead, otherwise he would have killed her!"

Then he dressed his old grandmother in her Sunday clothes, borrowed a neighbor's horse, hitched it to the carriage and put the old Grandmother up against the back seat so she could not fall out. Off they rode through the woods. At sunrise they came to a large inn and there Little Claus stopped to get a bite to eat.

The innkeeper had lots and lots of money. He was also a kind man, but he had a fiery temper and could explode as if there were pepper and snuff in him.

"Good morning!" he said to Little Claus, "My, you're a bit early to be in your Sunday best today, aren't you?"

"I know," said Little Claus, "I've got to go into town with my old Grandmother, she's sitting outside in the carriage and can't come in.

Would you be so kind to bring her a glass of mead? But you'll have to speak to her pretty loud because she's very hard of hearing."

"Yes, I'll be right along!" said the innkeeper and poured out a large glass of mead which he brought out to the dead Grandmother who had been propped up in the carriage.

"I've brought you a glass of mead from your grandson!" said the innkeeper, but the dead woman did not say a word. She just sat there silently.

"Didn't you hear me!" the innkeeper shouted as loud as he could, "I've brought you a glass of mead from your grandson!" Again and again he shouted the same thing, but as she did not even move from her seat, he grew angry and threw the glass right into her face. The mead ran down her nose and she tumbled over backwards in the carriage as she was only propped up and not fastened tightly.

"Hey!" shouted Little Claus, springing out of the door and grabbing the innkeeper by the throat, "You've just killed my Grandmother! Look at that big hole in her head!"

"Why, it was a terrible accident!" shouted the innkeeper, his hands trembling, "It's all because I've got such a bad temper! Dear Little Claus, I'll give you a whole bushelful of money and have your Grandmother buried just as if she were my own, but please don't tell anyone, otherwise they'll chop my head off, and that's so nasty!"

So once again Little Claus received a whole bushel full of money and the innkeeper buried the old Grandmother just as if she had been his own.

21

When Little Claus got home again with all the money, he quickly sent a boy over to Big Claus to ask him, if he could borrow a bushel.

"What's this?" said Big Claus, "didn't I kill him! I'd better go and check this out!" So he went over to Little Claus's with his bushel.

"Hey, where did you get all that money?" he asked. His mouth hung open in amazement at all the money Little Claus had.

"It was my Grandmother you killed and not me!" said Little Claus, "I've sold her for a bushelful of money!"

"You were well paid, I must say!" said Big Claus. He hurried home, took his axe and walloped his Grandmother over the head with it. Then he propped her up in his carriage and drove off into town where the undertaker lived and asked whether he would like to buy a dead body.

"Who is it and where did you get it from?" asked the undertaker.

"That's my Grandmother!" said Big Claus, "I killed her for a bushelful of money!"

"Good heavens!" said the undertaker.

"You're out of your mind! Don't say that kind of thing or you'll end up losing your head!" The undertaker told him he had done a terrible thing and what an evil person he was and how he ought to be punished. Big Claus became so frightened that he sprang straight into the carriage, whipping the horses and drove off home. All the people in town thought he was crazy. So they let him go his way.

"Now, you're in for it!" said Big Claus on his way home.

"You'll pay for this, Little Claus!" As soon as he reached home, he took the largest sack he could find, went over to Little Claus's and said, "You've tricked me again! First I killed all my horses, then my old Grandmother! And it's all your fault, you're not going to make a fool of me again!" So he grabbed hold of Little Claus and pushed him into the sack, slung it over his shoulder and shouted, "Now I'm going to drown you!"

There was a long way to go before he reached the river and Little Claus was not

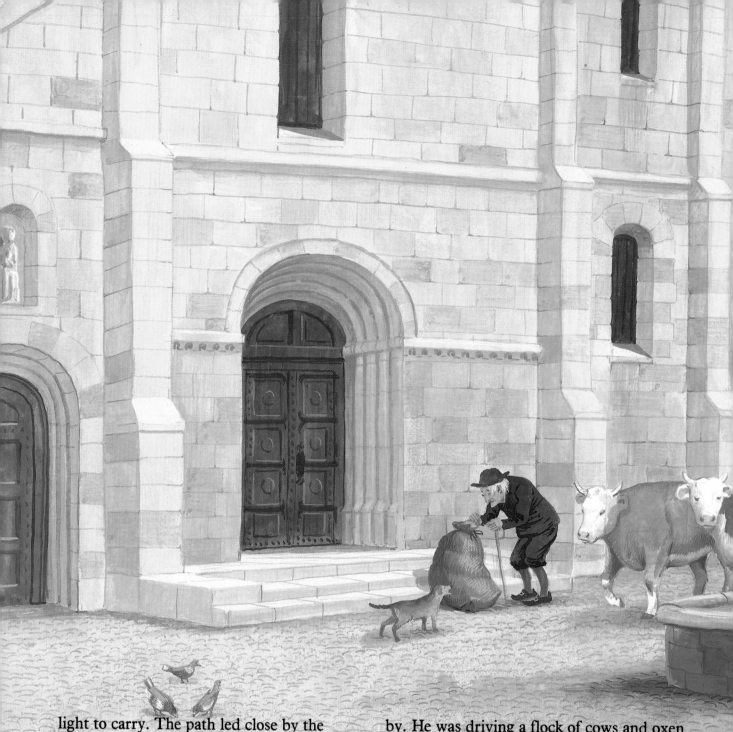

light to carry. The path led close by the church, the organ was playing and people were singing very cheerfully. So Big Claus put down his sack near the church door and thought how pleasant it would be just to go in and listen to a hymn before going any further. After all, Little Claus could not escape and all the people were in church, so he went inside.

"Oh dear! What a mess!" sighed Little Claus inside the sack, he twisted and wriggled all he could, but could not break loose.

At that moment an old herdsman with snow-white hair and a large staff in his hand came by. He was driving a flock of cows and oxen in front of him and they stumbled upon the sack Little Claus was in, knocking it over.

"Oh dear me!" sighed Little Claus, "I'm too young to die and go to heaven!"

"What about poor old me!" said the herdsman, "I'm so old and still I must wait until I get to heaven." "Open the sack!" shouted Little Claus, "change places with me and you'll soon get to heaven!"

"Oh yes, I'd like that very much!" said the herdsman.

He opened the sack and let Little Claus out.

"Will you look after my cattle?" said the old man as he crept into the sack, which Little Claus then tied. Little Claus said yes, then went on his way with the cows and oxen.

A little later Big Claus came out of church and swung the sack over his shoulder. Strangely enough it seemed like the sack had become lighter, for the old herdsman was not half as heavy as Little Claus. "He's not so heavy now! It's probably because I've heard a hymn!" Big Claus said.

He went to the river that was wide and deep, pushed the sack with the old herdsman into the water and shouted, "Ha! Now look where you are! Just you try and fool me again!" For he believed it was Little Claus he was throwing in the water.

Then he went on his way home, but as he reached the place where two paths crossed, he bumped into Little Claus who was driving all his cattle.

"What on earth!" said Big Claus, "didn't I drown you?"

"Sure you did!" said Little Claus, "Yes, you threw me in the river less than half an hour ago!"

"But wherever did you get all these fine cattle from?" asked Big Claus.

"They are sea-cattle!" said Little Claus, "Let me tell you the whole story. Thank you so much for drowning me, now I'm really becoming rich! I was so frightened inside the sack, the wind was howling past my ears when you threw me from the bridge into the cold water. I hit the bottom straight away, but I wasn't hurt, for down there grows the finest soft grass you can imagine.

As soon as I had landed on top of it, the sack was opened and the loveliest maiden dressed in chalk-white clothes with a green crown in her wet hair took me by the hand and said, "nice of you to drop in Little Claus! Here you are, have some cattle to begin with!

A mile up the road you'll find a whole ranch which you can have!" Then I saw that the river formed a large highway for the sea-people. Down on the seabed they walked and rode from the lake right to the land to where the river ends. There were so many beautiful flowers, the freshest grass and the fish swimming in the water darted past my ears,

just as if they were birds in the air. What lovely people and what splendid animals that grazed on the hills and the valleys!"

"But why have you come back up here again so soon?" asked Big Claus. "I wouldn't have done that if it was so pleasant down there!"

"Of course you would," said Little Claus "You see, I'm smart! As I told you, the sea maiden said that just a mile up the road, and by up the road she meant the river for she cannot travel any other way, there was yet another huge ranch of cattle just waiting for me. I know the course the river takes, sometimes turning this way, sometimes the other and it's quite a long way to go, so I decided to take a short cut by crossing over land and driving the cattle across to the river again, thereby saving nearly half a mile and reaching my sea-ranch a lot quicker!"

"What a lucky fellow you are!" said Big Claus, "Do you think I would also be given some sea-cattle when I reach the bottom of the river?"

"It wouldn't surprise me in the least!" said Little Claus, "But I can't carry you in the sack over to the river, you're far too heavy for me, but if you go over there yourself and get into the sack, it'll be my pleasure to throw you in!"

"Thanks very much!" said Big Claus, "but if I don't get any sea-cattle when I get down there, I'll give you a beating, you can be sure of that!"

"Oh come on, don't be so nasty!" Little Claus said. And on they went over towards the river. As the cattle, who by now were very thirsty, saw the water, they hurried as fast as they could to have a drink.

"Just see what a hurry they are in!" said Little Claus, "they can't wait to get back to the bottom again!"

"Come on, get a move on, help me into the sack!" said Big Claus, "or I'll give you a beating!"

And so he crept into the large sack, that had been lying over the backs of the oxen. "You'd better put a stone in with me, otherwise I'm afraid I might not sink to the bottom!" said Big Claus.

"That won't be any problem!" said Little Claus.

All the same, though, he put a large stone in the sack, tied the rope tightly and gave it a shove.

Plump! Straight away Big Claus sank to the bottom of the river. "I'm afraid he won't find any cattle down there!" said Little Claus who then went on his way home with all his cattle.

31

Little Claus and Big Claus

Explaining the story:

Since Big Claus was smarter and richer than Little Claus it looked as if he would win. Little Claus, on the other hand, was small and poor, but because he did not cheat, he became the winner, while Big Claus received no more than what he deserved.

3. Why was it wrong of Big Claus to say, "I'll pay you back for this!"? How did this promise end up hurting Big Claus more than Little Claus?

Talking about the truth of the story:

1. Why did Big Claus cheat? Didn't he think his wealth and size were enough to help him win?

2. In what ways did Big Claus act proud around Little Claus?

Applying the truth of the story:

1. When a person is mean to you, in what different ways might you react? What could happen as a result?

2. What kind of person would you like to become? How can you make that happen?